Noddy Builds a Rocket Ship

HarperCollins *Children's Books*

It was a lovely star-filled evening in Toyland.
Noddy was reading his new book.

"Zoom! Whoosh! Zap! Zow!"

"Wow this book on rocket ships is great!
I wish I had a rocket ship so I could travel to
the stars!" said Noddy.

Noddy looked out of the window at the stars in the sky.

"Hmm…" thought Noddy. "Maybe I could build a rocket ship…Yes! That's what I'll do! I'll build my own rocket ship!"

Noddy was so excited he ran into Toy Town to tell his friends.

On his way Noddy made up a song
to sing about rocket ships:

I'll have the best adventures
Of any toy you know
My rocket ship will take me anywhere I want to go
I'll travel to the planets
At quite a speedy pace

When I have built my rocket ship
I'll fly most every place
If you would like to join me
I'll take you flying soon
We'll spend the day in space and have
dinner on the moon

Noddy was so busy zooming along being
a rocket ship, that he didn't notice Martha
Monkey and Master Tubby Bear.

CRASH!

Noddy knocked his friends over.

"Ooops! Sorry, Martha Monkey. Sorry, Tubby
Bear," Noddy apologised.

Martha Monkey was not pleased. "Noddy!
What are you doing?" she asked, angrily.

"I'm being a rocket ship," replied Noddy.
"I'm going to build a rocket ship just like the one
in this book and zoom up into space."

Tubby Bear thought that sounded like a great
idea. "I'll help you, Noddy," he said. "If you let me
come along."

"Of course you can," said Noddy.

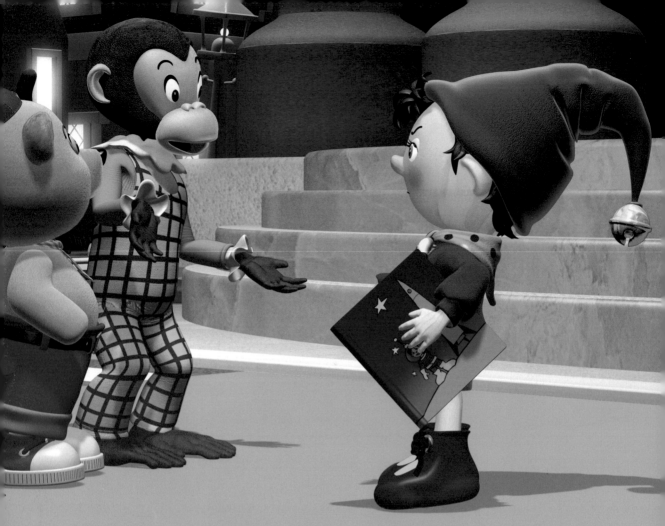

But Martha Monkey didn't think it could be done.
   "Rocket ships are built by very clever people,"
she said. "You two are silly if you think you can
build a rocket!"
   "But we will build a rocket ship!" Noddy
insisted. Noddy was certain he and Tubby Bear
could do it.

Noddy turned to Tubby Bear. "You believe me...
don't you?" he asked.

"Of course I do," Tubby replied. "I think we
could do anything!"

"We'll need help from someone who builds
things a lot," Noddy said, thoughtfully.

"I know!" cried Tubby Bear. "Mr Sparks!"

Noddy and Master Tubby Bear went to see Mr
Sparks at his garage.

"Building a rocket ship, eh?" asked Mr Sparks.
"That sounds like a challenge! I like it."

"Thank you, Mr Sparks," said Noddy, with a
smile. "But can you tell us how to start?"

Mr Sparks thought about how to build
a rocket ship.

"Well," began Mr Sparks. "You will need a pointy cone shape for the front. Then a tube shape for the middle. And finally three triangle shapes for the back."

"Will you help us find these shapes please, Mr Sparks?" asked Noddy.

Just then Clockwork Clown called Mr Sparks over to help fix his springs.

"You are welcome to use my tools, Noddy," called Mr Sparks. "But I have to help Clockwork Clown."

"Thanks, Mr Sparks," said Noddy. "It looks like we'll have to find the shapes for the rocket ship all by ourselves, Master Tubby Bear."

"Where will we find a pointy cone shape for the front of our rocket?" wondered Tubby Bear.

Noddy scratched his head and thought. "The cone shape will have to be like Clockwork Clown's hat…only bigger."

"The only cone shapes I know are ice cream cones," said Tubby Bear.

"That's it!" cried Noddy. "Well done, Tubby Bear. We should go and ask Miss Pink Cat at the Ice Cream Parlour if she can help us."

Miss Pink Cat was happy to help Noddy and Tubby Bear find the right shapes for their rocket ship. She gave them a double extra large ice cream cone!

"Wow!" gasped Noddy. "Thank you, Miss Pink Cat."

Noddy thought the cone would be perfect for the front of the rocket ship.

Tubby Bear thought the cone was perfect too.
Perfect for eating.

Tubby Bear was very disappointed that he
could not eat it straight away.

"Can I eat it after we've been in space,
Noddy?" he asked.

"Of course," said Noddy. "After we've
been to space."

Noddy thought about the list of parts Mr Sparks
had given them.

"Now we need a tube shape for the middle of
the rocket ship. Look, there's one!" Noddy called,
pointing to a lamppost.

"I don't think so, Noddy. It looks too skinny
for our rocket. What about that one?" Tubby
Bear pointed to an old rubbish bin.

"Well done, Tubby Bear," Noddy cheered. "And it doesn't look like anybody wants it."

But Mr Plod wasn't so sure that nobody would want the rubbish bin.

"What are you toys doing?" he asked, very sternly.

"We are building a rocket ship, Mr Plod," said Noddy. "We need this old bin for the middle."

"Very well then," said Mr Plod. "But stay out of trouble."

Noddy and Tubby Bear only had the triangle shapes to find. They went to Town Square to see if there was anything they could use.

"Hello!" called Dinah Doll. "What are you two up to?"

"Hello, Dinah!" replied Noddy. "We're building a rocket ship and the only parts we are missing are three triangles."

"Well you're in luck," said Dinah Doll. "I have some triangle shapes on my stall…Now just wait there while I find them."

Dinah Doll began to look around her stall for the triangle shapes.

"Here they are," she said, holding up three large triangles.

"Wow!" said Noddy and Tubby Bear. "These are perfect Dinah, thank you very much."

"Come on, Tubby Bear," shouted Noddy. "We can build our rocket ship now!"

Noddy and Tubby Bear were very busy in Mr Sparks' garage.

They put all their shapes on the table. The ice cream cone went at the front. They used the rubbish bin for the middle. The three triangle shapes from Dinah's stall went on the end.

"We make a great team, Tubby Bear," said Noddy. "Thank you for helping me to build my rocket ship."

"That's OK, Noddy," said Master Tubby Bear. "It was lots of fun!"

"Look, Noddy. Everybody has come to see your rocket ship fly!"

Mr Sparks had gathered everybody outside his garage to watch the rocket ship take off.

"Ladies and Gentlemen," said Mr Sparks, importantly. "I present to you Toy Town's first rocket ship."

Everybody cheered. Everybody except Martha Monkey.

"That's not a real rocket ship," said Martha. "It doesn't have a rocket motor to make it go!"

"Oh, no! She's right!" cried Noddy. "We were so busy getting all the shapes for the rocket we forgot about a motor!"

Big-Ears stepped forward. "Maybe I can help," he said.

"You have both worked so hard," said Big-Ears, kindly. "And you really believe this rocket ship will fly. I think a little magic might help."

Big-Ears sprinkled a little magic dust over the rocket ship.

"Wow!" gasped Noddy. "You jump-started our rocket! Thank you."

Zoooom!

The rocket ship shot up into the sky.
It went so high that Noddy and Tubby Bear could
touch the stars. Noddy picked a star to take to
Martha Monkey.

"Wheee!" shouted Master Tubby Bear. "This is
so much fun. What a great idea, Noddy!"

Back at Mr Sparks' garage everybody was
congratulating themselves on having helped to
find the right shapes for the rocket.

"Thank you all for helping to build our rocket
ship," smiled Noddy, as they landed. "But there is
one person who deserves a very special present."

Noddy gave the star he was holding to
Martha Monkey.

Noddy looked at Martha. "This is so you always remember to reach for the stars!"

Martha felt very bad for not believing in Noddy's rocket.

"Wow! Thanks, Noddy," she said. "That's a very special rocket ship. Um, any chance I could have a ride?"

Suddenly everybody wanted to ride Noddy's rocket.
"Don't worry," Noddy laughed. "Our new rocket
taxi will give everybody rides to the stars."

Everybody cheered, "Yaaaaay!" As Noddy and
Martha Monkey flew off into the sky.

First published in Great Britain by HarperCollins Children's Books in 2005
HarperCollins Children's Books is a division of HarperCollins Publishers Ltd,
77-85 Fulham Palace Road, Hammersmith, London W6 8JB

1 3 5 7 9 10 8 6 4 2

ISBN 0-00-721058-2

Printed and bound by
Printing Express Ltd, Hong Kong

make way for NODDY™

Collect them all!

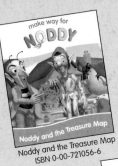

Noddy and the Treasure Map
ISBN 0-00-721056-6

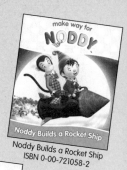

Noddy Builds a Rocket Ship
ISBN 0-00-721058-2

Noddy's Pet Chicken
ISBN 0-00-721057-4

Goblins Above
ISBN 0-00-721059-0

Hold on to Your Hat, Noddy
ISBN 0 00 712243 8

Noddy and the New Taxi
ISBN 0 00 712239 X

The Magic Powder
ISBN 0 00 715101 2

Bounce Alert in Toy Town
ISBN 0 00 715103 9

Noddy's Perfect Gift
ISBN 0 00 712365 5

A Bike for Big-Ears
ISBN 0 00 715105 5

And send off for your free Noddy poster (rrp £3.99).
Simply collect 4 tokens and complete the coupon below.

✂

TOKEN

Name: _____

Address: _____

_____

_____

e-mail: _____

❏ Tick here if you do not wish to receive further information about children's books.

Send coupon to: **Noddy Poster Offer, PO Box 142, Horsham, RH13 5FJ.**

Terms and conditions: proof of sending cannot be considered proof of receipt. Not redeemable for cash. 28 days delivery. Offer open to UK residents only.

Make Way For Noddy videos now available at all good retailers.

UNIVERSAL